Scribner
1230 Avenue of the
Americas
New York, NY 10020

to Nidol
T.M.

to Kali-Ma
S.M.

To Keith & Tom
P.L.

Many thanks to
P. Van Der Stricht,
president of
A. Merry Car
(Belgium)
P.L.

For INFORMATION regarding special discounts
for bulk purchases, please contact
Simon & Schuster Special Sales at
1-800-456-6798 or
business@simonandschuster.com

WHO'S GOT GAME?

Poppy or the Snake?

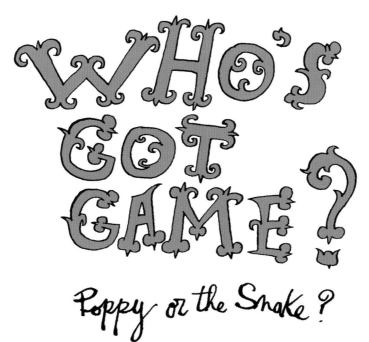

TONI & SLADE MORRISON
pictures by PASCAL LEMAITRE

SCRIBNER and design are trademarks of Macmillan Library Reference USA, Inc., used under license by Simon & Schuster, the publisher of this work.

DESIGNED by Pascal Lemaitre, colors by P. Lemaitre & E. Phuon.

Manufactured in the United States of America.
10 9 8 7 6 5 4 3 2 1

Graphix
J

Morrison
Main

Library of Congress Cataloging-in-Publication Data
Morrison, Toni.
        Poppy or the Snake? / Toni Morrison
                            and Slade Morrison;
        illustrated by Pascal Lemaitre.
    p. cm. — (Who's got game?)

1. Aesop's fables—Adaptations. 2. Fables, American.
I. Morrison, Slade. II. Lemaître, Pascal. III. Title.

    PS3563.O8749 P67 2004
    813'.54—dc21

                        2003042816

    ISBN: 0-7432-2249-0

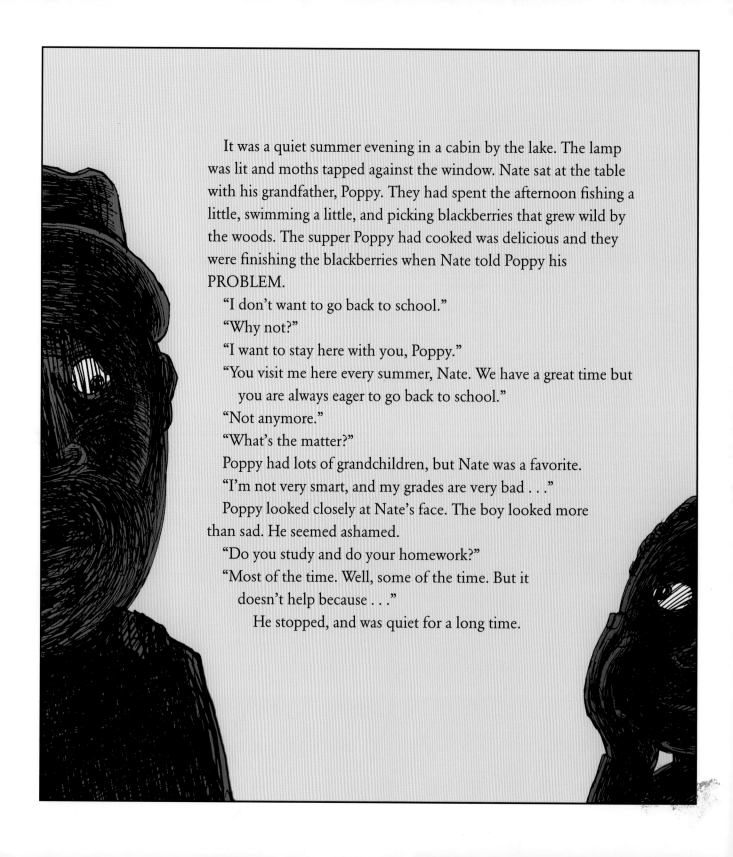

It was a quiet summer evening in a cabin by the lake. The lamp was lit and moths tapped against the window. Nate sat at the table with his grandfather, Poppy. They had spent the afternoon fishing a little, swimming a little, and picking blackberries that grew wild by the woods. The supper Poppy had cooked was delicious and they were finishing the blackberries when Nate told Poppy his PROBLEM.

"I don't want to go back to school."

"Why not?"

"I want to stay here with you, Poppy."

"You visit me here every summer, Nate. We have a great time but you are always eager to go back to school."

"Not anymore."

"What's the matter?"

Poppy had lots of grandchildren, but Nate was a favorite.

"I'm not very smart, and my grades are very bad . . ."

Poppy looked closely at Nate's face. The boy looked more than sad. He seemed ashamed.

"Do you study and do your homework?"

"Most of the time. Well, some of the time. But it doesn't help because . . ."

He stopped, and was quiet for a long time.

"Come on, you can tell me."

"Dad says I'm lazy. Mom says I don't concentrate."

"Which is it?"

"Both, I guess. I sit at my desk, but I can't seem to pay attention. There's so much going on that's more fun than schoolwork."

"I see."

Poppy thought awhile and then got up and went to the closet. He took out a pair of shiny boots. When he put them on, Nate asked, "Are you going out?"

"No. These are my remembering boots. They help me remember what I don't want to forget."

"How do they work?"

"Well, right now they're helping me remember that paying attention is just a way of taking yourself seriously."

"I don't understand."

Poppy cleared the dishes from the table. Then he turned down the lamp. When he sat down, both of their faces shone in the moonlight that flooded the room.

I drove out to the pier to fish one evening.

The weather was cool, and the fish were hungry. I caught several before it got too dark to see.

So I packed my gear and headed for my truck.

When I got there, I saw something caught under one of my tires. I reached down to pull it loose and discovered it wasn't a branch or a vine,...

...but a **SNAKE**.

I must have rolled over it when I parked. I took out my flashlight and pointed it toward the snake.

SUDDENLY, its eyes opened and its tail flicked. It scared me, so I shouted.

WHOA!

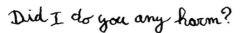
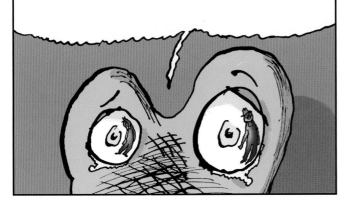

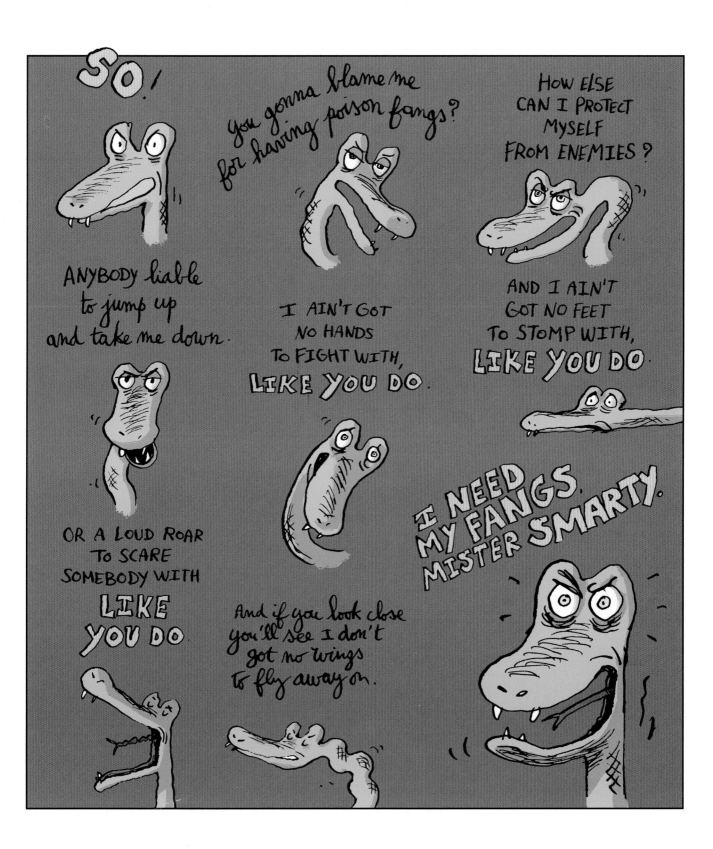

I got into the truck and started the engine. Slowly, I let the truck ease forward.

DID THAT DO IT?

What a relief!

Ahhh

The snake slid around a little to make sure all of him was together. He crawled close to the truck door, raised up, and opened his mouth.

Beautiful, dude.

BEAUTIFUL.

I'm glad it worked. I'll be off now.

OFF?

OFF WHERE?

HOME

I should have known you was a clown. I have to promise to be good, but you can drive on off. NEVER MIND WHAT YOU DONE.

I did what we agreed. What more do you want?

He slithered closer to my window.

I been pinned under your tire for hours. In pain, starving, scared out of my mind. And you mean to tell me you not going to take me home and give me something to eat?

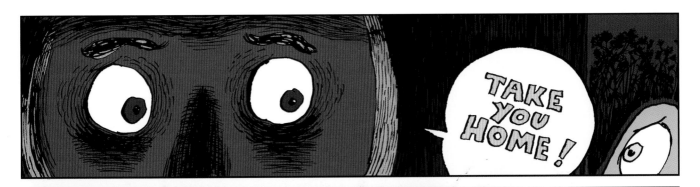

TAKE YOU HOME!

THAT'S RIGHT. OR IS THIS THE WAY YOU TREAT EVERYBODY YOU ROLL OVER AND ALMOST KILL?

BUT—

BUT WHAT? YOU SCARED? I SWORE I WOULDN'T EVEN THINK ABOUT BITING YOU. WOULD I WASTE MY POISON ON THE DUDE WHO SAVED ME, FED ME?

I thought about it and decided the snake meant what he said. There was no reason for him to bite a friend. So I picked him up and put him in the bed of the truck.

When we got to the cabin I filled a bowl with milk for him. Snake sipped until

it was all gone, and then, yawning, he curled up and went to sleep.

  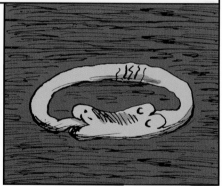

The next morning, at breakfast, I noticed Snake had bruises where the tire had struck him. Some of his scales had fallen off, and there were tiny scratches too. I got some medicine and woke him.

After a meal of toast and milk, Snake asked if he could stay another night. I had to smile. He had a sassy mouth, but he seemed like a good soul underneath.

SURE! STAY AWHILE.

After all, he'd sworn he wouldn't bite me, RIGHT?

I thought about that while I drove into the village.

I was late getting back, and when I opened the door, Snake...

"Not even a radio? You don't want no radio?"

"NO."

"Don't you get lonesome?"

"No."

"I like my own company."

"Is that right?"

Snake yawned and curled up on the mat near the stove.

I wasn't sleepy, so I sat on the porch and watched the stars for a while.

When I came back in, I noticed Snake had slithered closer to my bed to sleep. Early the next morning before the sun had risen... ⟶

... a sharp pain woke me. I sat up and saw two holes in my arm, pierced by a pair of fangs. I jumped up screaming. Snake was coiled on the blanket right in front of me. His fangs were shiny and dripping with poison.
LIAR! LIAR!

HEY, MAN. I'M A
SNAKE.

YOU KNEW THAT.

Poppy looked at Nate and laughed, slapping his knees. Nate stared at his grandfather. "What happened? You mean he bit you and you didn't die?"

"He bit me, all right. And no, I didn't die. You see, I thought about what snake had promised me. He said he wouldn't even think of biting me. He never said he wouldn't bite me—just that he wouldn't think of it. So I took a precaution and on the day I went to the village, I got a snake serum."

"Oh, that's what saved you!" Nate grinned.

"Not entirely. Paying attention is what saved me. And I never want to forget that, so I figured out a way to remember it."

Poppy turned up the lamp. He lifted his legs and stretched them out on the table.

Then, in the glow, Nate saw his grandfather's remembering boots. They were beautiful and made of the softest, shiniest snakeskin.